Teasing Tongue Twisters

picked by John Foster

Illustrated by Nathan Reed

Collins

An imprint of HarperCollins*Publishers*

First published by Collins in 2002
Collins is an imprint of HarperCollins*Publishers* Ltd,
77-85 Fulham Palace Road, Hammersmith, W6 8JB

The HarperCollins website address is:
www.**fire**and**water**.com

3 5 7 9 8 6 4

0 00 711214 9

Printed and bound in England by
Clays Ltd, St Ives plc

Teasing Tongue Twisters

Also compiled by John Foster

A Century of Children's Poems

Ridiculous Rhymes
Loopy Limericks
Dead Funny

The Pea Pod Poppers Pop

I'm not the pea pod popper,
I'm the pea pod popper's Pop.
I'm the seller, not the sheller,
Of popped peas, he pops for shops.

He pops peas for my selection,
For selling in my shops.
Pea pod popping to perfection,
Pea pod popping, for his Pop.

Ian Larmont

Dinosaur Diets

If a brontosaurus

ever stood before us,

it would simply explore us

and then – ignore us;

for in the stomach of a brontosaurus,

plants always came before us.

But if a tyrannosaurus

ever saw us,

it would simply adore us;

for in the stomach of a tyrannosaurus

is where they like to

STORE US!

Ian Souter

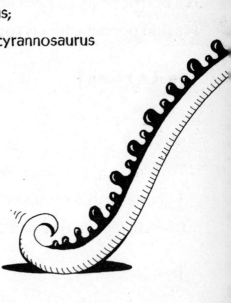

Dinah Shaw Saw a Dinosaur

Dinah Shaw saw a dinosaur.

The dinosaur saw Dinah Shaw.

The dinosaur that Dinah saw

Dined that night on Dinah Shaw.

Richard Caley

When Momma Laid the Table

When Momma laid the table
all the children cried in vain.
'No! Momma's laid the table
and it's marmalade again.'
'Please pass a pear,' called Poppa.
'No, on second thoughts, pass two.
A pair of pears,' said Poppa,
'yes, a pair of pears will do.'
'I'd like a plaice,' said Aunty.
'Place a plaice upon my plate.
A piece of plaice placed in
my place, with chips would be just great.'
'But Momma laid the table,'
went the children's sad refrain,
'and it's mommalaid, no, marmalade
for each of us again.'

Marian Swinger

High Rise King Size Super Duper Snack

King prawn mushroom bacon double cheddar
Char grilled fish filled chicken double header
Marmalade marinade A-grade beef
Toffee coated nut brittle crunchy on the teeth.

Triple decker pickled pepper griddled rack of rib
Battered wedge curried veg peanut satay dip
Deep filled flame grilled meat meat meat
Between big bread buns — a tangy tasty treat.

The bigger and the beefier the burger is the better
A fast food snack attack appetite whetter
A jack 'em up pack 'em up rack 'em up stack
A high rise king size super duper snack.

Paul Cookson

If a Ghoul is Fond of Goulash

If a ghoul is fond of goulash,

Is the ghoul a little foolish,

Should he feel, if full of goulash,

As a ghoul he's not so ghoulish?

Colin West

Two Toucans

How can two toucans open two cans?
Two toucans can open two cans
with two can-openers.

Jane Clarke

Gregory Gruber

Gregory Gruber, gargantuan glutton
would gobble green gooseberries, gumbo and
  mutton.
He'd gurgle down gravy, gulp garlic galore
then like a great gannet, would gullet some more.
'Oh, glorious grub,' he would gasp. 'Give me grease,
give me gobstoppers, gristle. (He gave us no
  peace.)
Give me gollops of gruel and gobbets of goose,
grill it and garnish it, glaze it. And juice,
give me gallons and gallons to gulp and to glug
and give it to me in a gardener's trug.'
Gregory Gruber grew gross as he guzzled.
Poor Gregory Gruber shoud've been muzzled
for that great gourmadister's gut overloaded
and Gregory Gruber (we warned him) exploded.

Marian Swinger

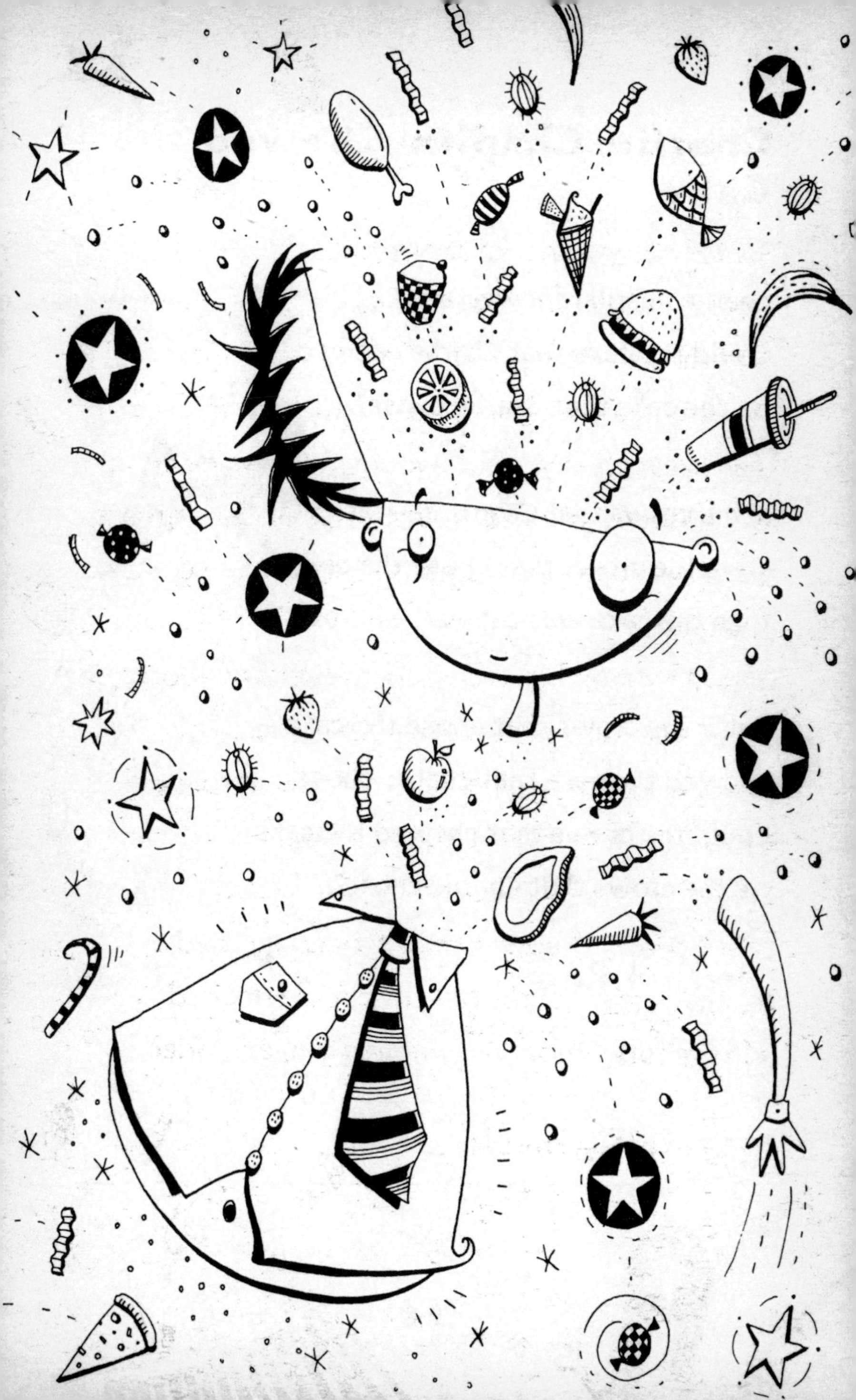

Charlie Chaplin Chewed a Cake

Charlie Chaplin chewed a cake.
Could the cake that Charlie chewed
be the cake that Charlie chose?

If the crows that Charlie caught
were the crows that chose the cake
then the cake was chewed by crows.

But if the crows that chose the cake
chewed the cake that Charlie chose,
could the crows that chewed the cake
be the crows that Charlie chose?

Michael Rosen

To Slim or Not to Slim

Uncle Slim said to Jim:

'You're too fat. You should slim.'

'Who?' said Jim. 'You,' said Slim. 'Me?' said Jim,

'I'm too fat?' 'Yes,' said Slim.

'I'm not fat,' answered Jim,

'If I slim, I'll be thin, Uncle Slim.'

At that moment Old Jim

Came along. 'Jim,' said Slim,

'Don't you think Jim should slim?' 'What?' said Jim,

'Jim should slim?' 'Yes,' said Slim.

'No,' said Jim, 'not young Jim,

If Jim slims, he'll be slimmer than Slim.'

'Who?' said Slim. 'Slim,' said Jim,

'Not you, Slim, but young Slim.'

'Oh,' said Slim, 'Slim's much slimmer than Jim.'

'Yes,' said Jim. 'Slim's too slim.'

'Who's too slim, Jim?' said Jim.

'Slim's too slim, Jim,' said Jim. 'Yes,' said Slim.

'Here he comes!' cried Old Jim.

'Who?' said Slim. 'Not young Slim?'

'Yes,' said Jim. 'Hallo Slim.' 'Hallo Jim.'

'Slim, Slim thinks Jim should slim.'

'No, Jim's slim, aren't you, Jim?'

'Yes, Slim.' 'Yes,' said Slim. 'Jim, Slim, Jim, swim?'

Richard Edwards

Poppy's Frothy Coffee

Poppy makes rather frothy coffee
In a proper copper-bottomed coffee pot.
For a proper copper-bottomed coffee maker
Keeps rather frothy coffee properly hot.

Cynthia Rider

A Proper Copper Kettle

I took a proper copper kettle
To the top of Popocatepetl.
And on the top of Popocatepetl
I put my proper copper kettle.

Colin West

Sitting Sipping Sarsaparilla

She was sitting sipping sarsaparilla
slowly through a straw,
sipping, sighing sadly on
a sweeping sandy shore.
Seagulls, shrieking, swooped in circles.
Sea spray speckled stones
were submerged as surf surged seething,
settling where she sat, alone.
She sat silent, sea surrounded
till, the sarsaparilla gone
she swam, a sea sprite, swiftly seawards.
A setting sun shone soft upon
her scaled tail, shedding silver sea spray,
which slapped the sea, swish, smack! The sound
scared the seagulls who swept, screaming
in swirling spirals all around.

Marian Swinger

A Twister for Two Tongues

'I can can-can.

Can you can-can?'

'Yes, I can can-can too.

In fact, I can can-can

Very, very well.

I can can-can better than you.'

'No, you can't can-can

better than I can can-can

because I can can-can better!'

'Bet you can't!'

'Bet I can!'

'Bet you can't!'

'Bet I can! I can! I can can-can better!'

Cynthia Rider

Moses Supposes

Moses supposes his toeses are roses,
But Moses supposes erroneously;
For nobody's toeses are posies of roses
As Moses supposes his toeses to be.

Anon

Crazy Clarence Clack

'Clone me!' Clarence Clack commanded his
   computer.
'Clone me countless Clarence Clacks or be crashed.'

'Oh, cruel, cruel Clack,' complained the computer,
craftily calculating.

'I crave Clacks,' crooned crazy Clarence.
'Create me Clacks. Create me a colony of Clacks,
a camp of Clacks, a cohort of Clacks,
a cacophony of Clacks,
crusty Clacks, copy Clacks,
cuddly Clacks, cantankerous Clacks,
King Clacks, Clacks of all classes,
a Cosmos crammed with Clacks.'

COPY

The computer clicked, clacked, clunked,
and created Clacks.
A cornucopia of Clacks cascaded,
cursing, colliding, kicking and clamouring.
'Cor!' cackled Clarence
clapping, cavorting and capering.

But a carpet of Clacks collected,
converging, congealing,
clutching, crushing Clarence Clack.
'Cretins! Clods! Clots! Criminals!'
cried Clarence Clack crumpling.
Then, clawing cravenly,
he croaked his last.

The crafty computer created itself King of Clacks
and later, conquered the world.

Marian Swinger

Esau Wood Sawed Wood

Esau Wood sawed wood.
Esau Wood would
saw wood.
Oh, the wood that
Wood would saw!
One day Esau Wood
saw a saw saw wood
as no other woodsaw
Wood ever saw
would saw wood.
Of all the woodsaw
Wood ever saw saw
wood, Wood never
saw a woodsaw that
would saw wood
like the woodsaw
Wood saw would
saw wood. Now
Esau Wood saws with
that saw he saw saw wood.

Anon

I Saw Esau

I saw Esau kissing Kate.
Fact is, we all three saw.
I saw Esau, he saw me,
And she saw I saw Esau.

Anon

Who'll Go, If You'll Go

Do you know Hugo?
He'll go if I'll go
And Hugh'll go, if you'll go.
So... Hugo'll go and Hugh'll go
If I go and you go
That's who'll go, if you'll go.

John Foster

Six Sick Sikhs Met Six Sick Sheiks

Six sick Sikhs met six sick sheiks.

'Shake hands,' said the Sikhs.

'Shake hands,' said the sheiks.

'We're sick of being sick,'

said the six sick Sikhs.

'We're sick of being sick,'

said the six sick sheiks.

Six Sikhs with the shivers.

Six sheiks with the shakes.

John Foster

Hugh Hughes' Shoes

Hugh Hughes' shoes are huge shoes.
Huge are the shoes that Hugh Hughes uses.
Hugh is a youth whose shoes are huge.
Huge are the shoes in which Hugh Hughes cruises.

When Hugh Hughes queues to view new shoes
blue is the hue Hugh'll usually choose.
Few are the shoes Hugh'll choose to peruse.
Shoes are refused that are not truly huge.

A blue suit suits Hugh Hughes' huge shoes.
In a smooth blue suit and his new blue shoes
(shoes surely as huge as two blue canoes)
he's a truly cool dude is groovy Hugh Hughes!

David Horner

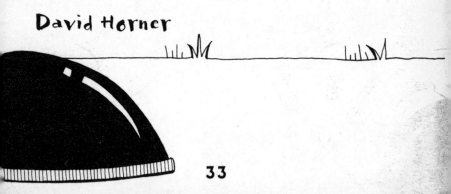

Underwood's Underwear

Underwood would wear underwear
If Underwood knew where
Underwood put
Underwood's underwear.

Did Underwood put his underwear
Under here or over there?
Did Underwood put his underwear
Under or over the chair?

I wonder, wonder where,
Underwood put
Underwood's underwear?

Louisa Fairbanks

Three Thriftless Threshers

Three thriftless threshers
Threshing the corn
Threw all their thandwiches
Into the bourne.

Thome of them floated,
Thome of them thank,
Tho three thriftless threshers
Thlid down the bank.

One lotht hith Thermoth Flathk,
One lotht hith thoes,
The third one wath naked
Tho had nothing to lothe.

Pam Gidney

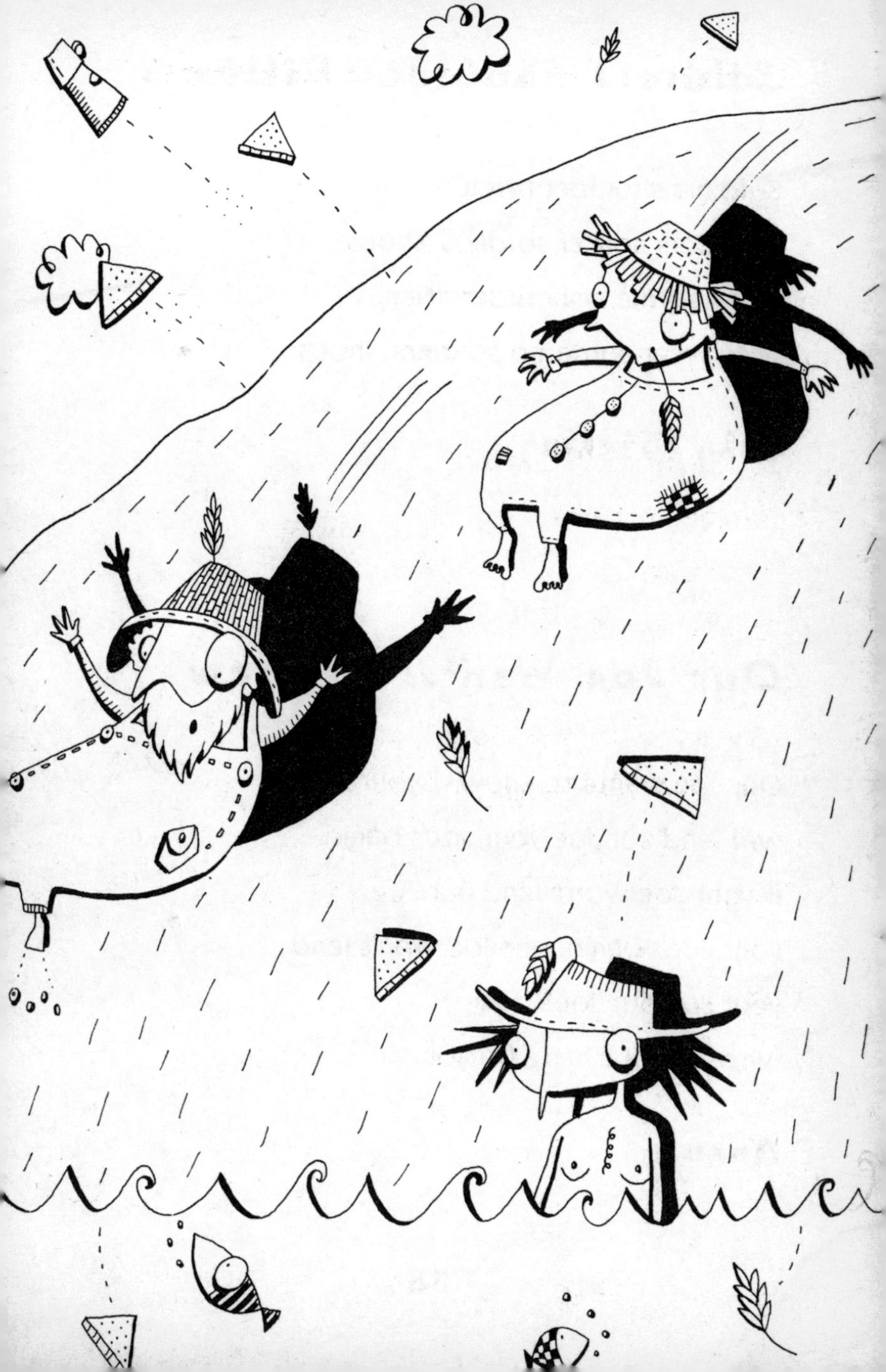

Soldiers Shoulder Rifles

Soldiers shoulder rifles.

Cobblers solder soldiers' shoes.

When soldiers shoulder rifles,

They wear soldered soldiers' shoes.

John Kitching

Our Joe Wants to Know

Our Joe wants to know if your Joe

will lend our Joe your Joe's banjo.

If your Joe won't lend our Joe

your Joe's banjo, our Joe won't lend

your Joe our Joe's banjo

when our Joe has a banjo!

Anon

Mr Lott's Allotment

Mr Lott's allotment
Meant a lot to Mr Lott.
Now Mr Lott is missed a lot
On Mr Lott's allotment.

Colin West

Jumble Jingle

Pick up a stick up,
    A stick up now pick;
Let me hear you say that
    Nine times, quick!

Laura E. Richards

Shaun Short's Short Shorts

Shaun Short bought some shorts.

The shorts were shorter than Shaun Short thought.

Shaun Short's short shorts were so short,

Shaun Short thought *Shaun, you ought*

Not to have bought shorts so short.

John Foster

Sheila Shorter Sought a Suitor

Sheila Shorter sought a suitor;
Sheila sought a suitor short.
Sheila's suitor's sure to suit her;
Short's the suitor Sheila sought!

Anon

Sue Shore Shrieked

Sue Shore shrieked.
Sue Shore shouted 'Shoo!'
Sue was sure she saw
A shrew in her shoe.

Derek Stuart

Antonio

Antonio, Antonio,
Was tired of living alonio.
 He thought he would woo
 Miss Lissamy Lou,
Miss Lissamy Lou Molonio.

Antonio, Antonio,
Rode off on his polo-ponio.
 He found the fair maid
 In a bowery shade,
A-sitting and knitting alonio.

Antonio, Antonio,
Said, 'If you will be my ownio
 I'll love you true,
 And I'll buy for you,
An icery creamery conio!'

'Oh, nonio, Antonio,
You're far to bleak and bonio!
    And all that I wish,
    You singular fish,
Is that you'll quickly begonio.'

Antonio, Antonio,
He uttered a dismal moanio;
    Then ran off and hid
    (Or I'm told that he did)
In the Antartical Zonio.

Laura E. Richards

First Ride

Professor Percy Postlethwaite
perched on his penny farthing
preens and poses;
pushes off.

Proceeds precariously
past 'Patterson's Pies'
and the Co-op .
              .
            .
          .
        .
      .

    pedals .
          .
        .
      .
    .

    puffing, panting
    puffing, panting
    perspiring
    profusely
    to the peak
    of Primrose Hill.

Teeters

totters

can't touch down a toe

to go slow

but tears downhill

full tilt

on tinpot wheels

ter-ump, ter-ump, ter-ump

over the cobbles,

the kerb;

pelts through the portals

of Prince's Park,

presses a bed of

purple pansies flat and –

AAAARGH!!!

Look, mama, lisps little Lizzie Lumpkin.
Look at Pwofethor Pofflewaite
paddling in the pond!

Patricia Leighton

bang!

Reckless Racing

Reckless Rick's
reckless racing
recklessly wrecked
Rick's red racer.

Reckless Rick's
reckless racing
ricked Rick's neck
and wrecked Rick's racer.

Jane Clarke

Dry Slope Skiing

Di dry skis on a dry ski slope
Dry slope skiing on a dry ski slope
Slalom skiing on a dry ski slope
Dry Di dry skis dry ski slopes.

Paul Cookson

How to Say Antartica

An

Ark

An Arc

An Arc Kick

Ant

Art

Ant Art

Anti-Arty

Arty Auntie

Ant

Art

Ant Art

Ant Ark Tick

Ant Arc Tickle

Ant

Arc

Antarc

Antarc Tick

Antartic... Ah!

Antarctica

Mary Green

Samual Swordfish

Samuel Swordfish Swimmer Supreme
Sports a subtle, striped, swimsuit
Swish as you've seen.
Swivelling, swirling,
Sweeping, swimming
A swaggering symbol of a suave, swinging,
   swimmer.
But any swordfish sporting a striped swimsuit
Subtle or otherwise
Should be under surveillance
On suspicion of stalking
All the shimmering shoals of shellfish in the sea.

Margaret Blount

Frank Tate's Tank Freight

Frank Tate's Tank Freight
Freights Frank's tanks
The freight Frank's tanks freight
Are tanks from France.

The weight Frank's tanks weigh
Makes Frank's freight weight
The tank's weight Frank takes
Weights Frank's freight.

Frank's tanks freight weights
The freight weight Tate's take
Frank Tate's Tank Freight
Tanks Frank's freight.

Frank Tate Tank Freight
Freights Frank's tanks
The freight Frank's tank freight
Are tanks from France.

Paul Cookson

Why Barnacles Cling to Boats

Boats bob about, banging their bottoms on
   barnacles,
And barnacles bang the bottoms of boats
   bobbing about –
So, sometimes barnacles cling to a boat's bobbing
   bottom,
And the banging boat bottom becomes a bobbing
   barnacle base!

Coral Rumble

Sipping Cider on the Zuyder Zee

She wallowed in the Zuyder Zee,

The breeze had ceased to spank;

The crew of her was him and me,

A Dutchman and a Yank.

Inside her there was cider, there was cider in the

    sea,

And cider on the starboard side, the larboard side,

    the lee,

And much of such inside the Dutch, and much of

    such in me.

From starboard spake the Dutchman, and full

    merrily spake he;

'The starboard is the steer-board side, so steer me

    two or three;

And when we've sipped the cider, we will sip the

    cider sea.'

From larboard then the Yankee spake, the Yankee
   being me,
'The larboard is the loading side, so load in two or
   three.
We'll sip up all the cider, see, and then the Zuyder
   Zee.'

Willard R. Espy

Anteater Anita

Peter anteater
Met anteater Rita
And now there's anteater Anita.

Mary Green

Once Upon a Barren Moor

Once upon a barren moor
There dwelt a bear, also a boar;
The bear could not bear the boar;
The boar thought the bear a bore.
At last the boar could bear no more
The bear that bored him on the moor,
And so one morn the bear he bored –
The bear will bore the boar no more.

Anon

Should You Meet a Herd of Zebras

Should you meet a herd of Zebras,
And you cannot tell the hebras
Of the Zebras from the shebras –
Watch which way each Zebra peebras.

Dick King-Smith

I Wannabe a Wallaby

I wannabe a wallaby,
A wallaby that's true.
Don't wannabe a possum
A koala or a roo.

I wannago hop hopping
Anywhere I please.
Hopping without stopping
Through eucalyptus trees.

A wallaby, a wallaby
Is what I wannabe.
I'd swap my life to be one,
But a problem – I can see;

If I'm gonna be a wallaby
I shall have to go and see
If I can find a wallaby,
A very friendly wallaby,
Who would really, really, really...
Wannabe... ME!

David Whitehead

Tongue-Twisting Couplets

Shapely swordfish in shallow shoals
shift shivering shellfish from shell holes.

Tentatively titivating, Treena Trees
tries twenty T-shirts, trying to please.

Burping Beppo bottles bad beer,
flat and foully flavoured, I fear...

Proper, portly politicians
put preposterous propositions.

Glowering Gloria's gloomy glances
rarely result in ripe romances.

Ghastly Grandpa's gurgling grog,
Greedy Greg grumbled, grudgingly agog.

Slithery snakes, slimily sliding,
celebrate Snake Swamp's surviving.

Michael Dugan

Sloth

A succulent slob of a slug
slept in a sewer, so snug,
he slipped in his sleep
down a slope, sort of steep,
and sank in the slime with a shrug.

Gina Douthwaite

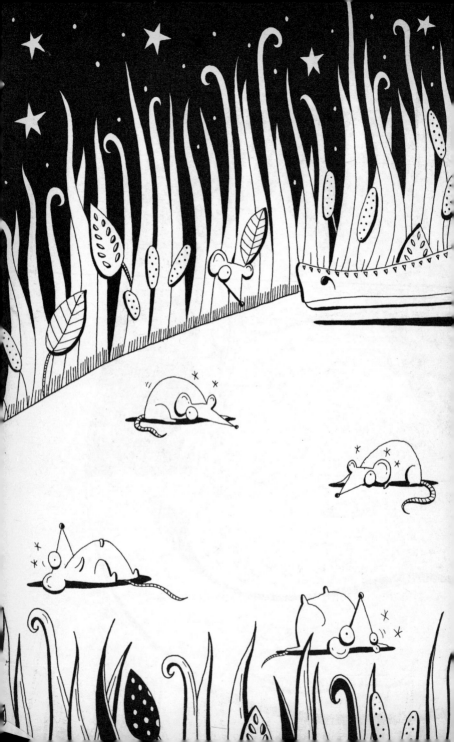

Wally the Wascally Weptile

Wally was a weptile,
a weally wotten one;
he'd wun awound the swamp at night
doing howwid things for fun.

He'd wush between the wushes
chasing swamp-wats wound and wound,
until the wats got tiad
and collapsed upon the ground.

Then he'd wam the wabbits
from the meadows to the wivah,
and woll awoud with laughtah,
as the wabbits shook and shivahed.

Yes. Wally was a weptile,
a weally wotten one,
until one day when he at last
was gwounded by his mum.

His mum said, 'Wally, weally,
I just can't believe it's twue.
My fwiends awound the swamp weport
such howwid things of you.'

She said, 'My son, I'll gwound you.

Stay inside fowevah!

Wascally weptiles such as you

awe weally not that clevah.'

She told him, 'No mo' wunning,

no mo' wushing at the wats

o'wamming wabbits into wivahs,

'cause they weally don't like that.'

Now Wally's still a weptile,

and he's still a wotten one.

But he's sowwy 'bout wushing and wamming,

'cause now he can't have any fun.

Aislinn and Larry O'Loughlin

Announcing the Guests at the Space Beasts' Party

'The Araspew from Bashergrannd'

'The Cakkaspoo from Danglebannd'

'The Eggisplosh from Ferrintole'

'The Gurglenosh from Hiccupole'

'The Inkiblag from Jupitickle'

'The Kellogclag from Lamandpickle'

'The Mighteemoose from Nosuchplace'

'The Orridjuice from Piggiface'

'The Quizziknutt from Radishratt'

'The Splattersplut from Trikkicatt'

'The Underpance from Verristrong'

'The Willidance from Xrayblong'

'The Yuckyspitt from Ziggersplitt'

Wes Magee

The Modern Hiawatha

He killed the noble Mudjokovis,

With the skin he made him mittens,

Made them with the fur side inside,

Made them with the skin side outside,

He, to get the warm side inside,

Put the inside skin side outside:

He, to get the cold side outside,

Put the warm side fur side inside:

That's why he put the fur side inside,

Why he put the skin side outside,

Why he turned them inside outside.

George A. Strong

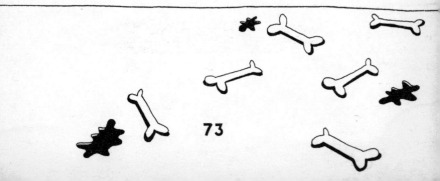

Underwood the Undertaker

Underhill, the master baker,

Asked Underwood the undertaker

To undertake an undertaking.

'I'll undertake your undertaking,'

Said Underwood the undertaker,

'On the understanding that I'm making

An exception by taking

On this undertaking.

'Cause if I'm not mistaken

This undertaking that I'm taking

Is the hardest undertaking

That I've ever undertaken.'

Derek Stuart

Weather

Whether the weather be fine
Or whether the weather be not,
Whether the weather be cold
Or whether the weather be hot,
We'll weather the weather
Whatever the weather,
Whether we like it or not.

Anon

Peter Potter's Portrait Posters

Peter Potter painted portraits,

Put the portraits onto posters,

Pinned the posters to his gatepost.

Patty Porter saw the portraits,

Said to Peter Potter, 'Please

Paint my portrait on a poster.

So

  Peter Potter painted Patty Porter's

  portrait and put it on a poster

And

  Patty Porter pinned Peter Potter's

  poster on her gatepost.

John Foster

Truanting, Of Course

Tanya's teacher taught a trio of troublesome truants.

Did Tanya's teacher teach a trio of troublesome truants?

If Tanya's teacher taught a trio of troublesome truants,

Where's the trio of troublesome truants

Tanya's teacher taught?

Andrea Shavick

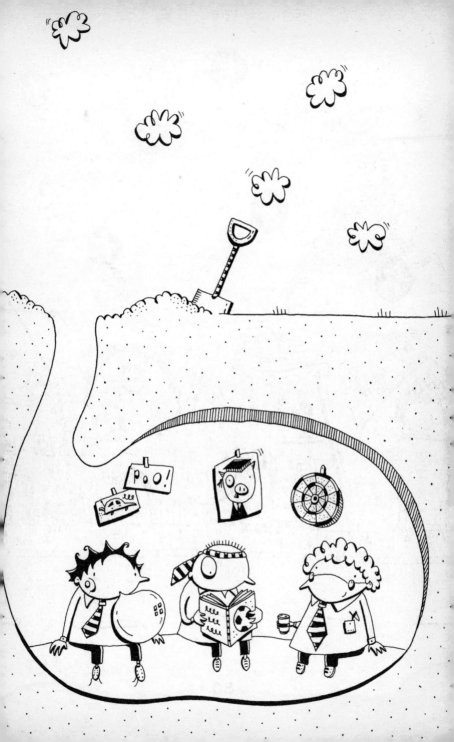

Skateboard Speeder

To swerve the streets at sundown with the night
   nip near
On witchy wonder wheels in his green-glo gear
Past pop-eyed people pointing at the disappearing
   dart
Of the shin-skinned skimmer with a hip-hop heart!

J. Patrick Lewis

Shut the Shutter

'Go, my son, and shut the shutter,'
This I heard a mother utter.
'Shutter's shut,' the boy did mutter.
'I can't shut'er any shutter.'

Anon

Sue Shore Shrieked

Sue Shore shrieked.
Sue Shore shouted 'Shoo!'
Sue was sure she saw
A shrew in her shoe.

Derek Stuart

You've No Need to Light a Night Light

You've no need to light a night light
On a light night like tonight,
For a night light's light's a slight light
And tonight's a night that's light.
When a night's light, like tonight's light,
It is really not quite right
To light night lights with their slight lights
On a light night like tonight.

Anon

Quite Right, Mrs Wright

On the night before the first night of *Twelfth Night*
Dwight Wright had stagefright,
And Mrs Wright said, 'Don't get uptight, Dwight,
It'll be all right on the night.'

On the night after the first night of *Twelfth Night*
Dwight Wright said, 'In spite
Of being uptight with stagefright, it went all right.
You were quite right, Mrs Wright.'

John Foster

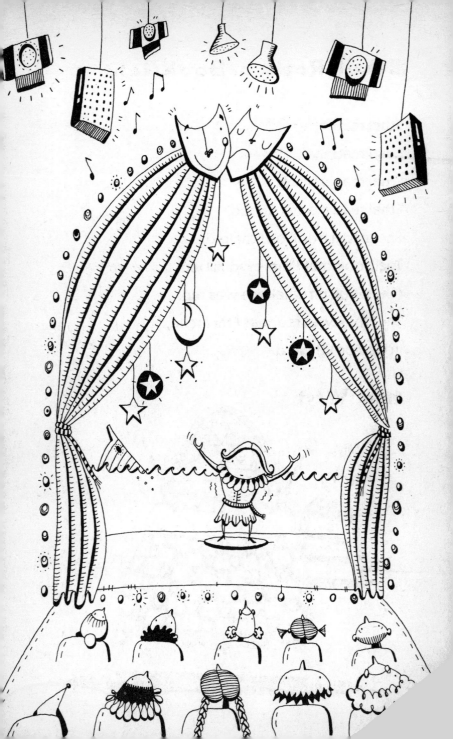

Ethel Read a Book

Ethel read,

Ethel read,

Ethel read a book.

Ethel read a book in bed.

She read a book on Ethelred.

The book that Ethel read in bed,

(The book on Ethelred) was red.

The book was red that Ethel read,

In bed on Ethelred.

Colin West

Tell Me Another One

A tall-tale teller
And a tell-tale teller
Told tales together.
The tall-tale teller
Said his were true.
'Oooo,' said the tell-tale teller,
'I'll tell on you.'
And he did.

Catherine Benson

A Wise Child Knows His Own Nose

'If you want a good spell,' the magician said,
'one that helps you write words right,
you must read a red book in reeds till it's read
and wait at night till a knight comes in sight
then weigh his weight at a way-side site
and drop a pail on his pale head.

'You must meet a bear and see the sea
and eat bare meat and be a bee
you must hear a tale without a flaw
and saw a tail that isn't sore,
knead flowers to flour, flee from a flea,
and stare at stairs here on the floor.

'You need to know when to say no,
which week is weak, which witch is not,
which rain is quick, which rein is slow,
which herd is heard, which wood would rot –
which tide is tied into a knot –
That's it,' he sighed, 'I've spelled the lot.'
And he threw me through the window.

Dave Calder

Tonight's Web Site

Have you visited The White Kite's night flight web
   site?
No, I haven't visited The White Kite's night flight
   web site
But tonight I might if my dad says it's all right
To visit The White Kite's night flight web site.

John Coldwell

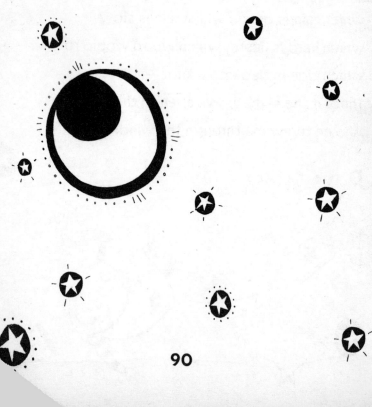

Night Mer

One night when I was fast apeels
all duggled snown and warm
I had a very dasty ream
about a stunder thorm
and fightning lashed
and saves at wea
like boiling werpents sithed
and foaming angs did frockle me
and shicked and slucked and eyethed.
They ulled me under, lungings full
of fevvered, fluffin fug
till suffing grably I apized
upon the redboom bug.

Gina Douthwaite

Ox and Axolotl

I had a little ox
And a little axolotl
I liked my axolotl lots
I liked my ox a little
My ox lived in a little box
My axolotl in a bottle
Box and bottle both lacked locks
I lost my ox and axolotl

Paul Bright

Talkative Cows

Have you heard the tittle-tattle
From a chatty herd of cattle?

Chewing cud and chewing fat'll
Set the tongues of cows a-rattle.

Each'll natter, each'll prattle,
Chatter like a diplomat'll.

When they row, there's little that'll
End their bitter verbal battle.

So, if you can hush these cattle,
I'll not only eat my hat, I'll
Swim from Scarborough to Seattle.

Nick Toczek

The Tongue-Twister

Watch out for the dreaded Tongue-twister
When he pulls on his surgical gloves.
Keep your eyes open, your mouth tightly shut,
Twisting tongues is the thing that he loves.

It's the slippery, squirmy feel of them
As they wriggle like landed fish.
When he pulls and tugs and grapples
You'll gasp and gurgle and wish

That you'd never pulled tongues at teacher
Or a stranger behind their back,
As he twists out your tongue and pops it
Into his bobbling, twisted-tongue sack.

Roger McGough

Acknowledgements

We are grateful to the following authors for permission to include the following poems, all of which are published for the first time in this collection:

Catherine Benson: 'Tell Me Another One' copyright © Catherine Benson 2002; Margaret Blount: 'Samuel Swordfish' copyright © Margaret Blount 2002; Paul Bright: 'Ox and Axolotl' copyright © Paul Bright 2002; Dave Calder: 'A Wise Child Knows His Own Nose' copyright © Dave Calder 2002; Richard Caley: 'Dinah Shaw Saw a Dinosaur' copyright © Richard Caley 2002; Jane Clarke: 'Two Toucans', 'Shy Shorn Sheep' and 'Reckless Racing' copyright © Jane Clarke 2002; John Coldwell: 'Tonight's Web Site' copyright © John Coldwell 2002; Paul Cookson: 'High Rise King Size Super Duper Snack', 'Frank Tate's Tank Freight' and 'Dry Slope Skiing' all copyright © Paul Cookson 2002; Gina Douthwaite: 'Sloth' copyright © Gina Douthwaite 2002; Louisa Fairbanks: 'Underwood's Underwear' copyright © Louisa Fairbanks 2002; John Foster: 'Six Sick Sikhs Met Six Sick Sheiks', 'Sean Short's Short Shorts', 'Peter Potter's Portrait Posters', 'Who'll Go if You'll Will Go' and 'Quite Right, Mrs Wright' all copyright © John Foster 2002; Pam Gidney 'Three Thiftless Threshers' copyright © Pam Gidney 2002; Mary Green: 'How to say Antarctica' and 'Anteater Anita' both copyright © Mary Green 2002; David Horner: 'Hugh Hughes' Shoes' copyright © David Horner 2002; John Kitching: 'Soldiers Shoulder Rifles' copyright © John Kitching 2002; Ian Larmont: 'The Pea Pod Poppers Pop' copyright © Ian Larmont 2002; J. Patrick Lewis: 'Skateboard Speeder' copyright © J. Patrick Lewis 2002; Patricia Leighton: 'First Ride' copyright © Patricia Leighton 2002; Wes Magee: 'Announcing the Guests at the Space Beasts' Party' copyright © Wes Magee 2002; Roger McGough 'The Tongue Twister' copyright © Roger McGough 2002. Reprinted by permission of PFD on behalf of Roger McGough; Cynthia Rider: 'Poppy's Frothy Coffee' and 'A Twister for Two Tongues' copyright © Cynthia Rider 2002; Andrea Shavick: 'Truanting, Of Course' copyright © Andrea Shavick 2002; Ian Souter: 'Dinosaur Diets' copyright © Ian Souter 2002; Derek Stuart: 'Underwood the Undertaker' and 'Sue Shore Shrieked' all copyright © Derek Stuart 2002; Marian Swinger: 'When Momma Laid the Table', 'Gregory Gruber', 'Sitting Sipping Sarsaparilla' and 'Crazy Clarence Clack' all copyright © Marian Swinger 2002; David Whitehead: 'I Wannabe a Wallaby' copyright © David Whitehead 2002.

We also acknowledge permission to include previously published poems:

Gina Douthwaite: 'Night Mer' copyright © Gina Douthwaite 1998, first published in Unzip Your Lips compiled by Paul Cookson (Macmillan), included by permission of the author; Michael Dugan: 'Tongue Twisting Couplets', included by permission of the author; Willard R.Espy: 'Sipping Cider on the Zuyder Zee' from A Children's Almanac of Words at Play by Willard R. Espy, copyright © Willard R. Espy 1982. Used by permission of Clarkson. N. Potter, a division of Random House, Inc; Richard Edwards: 'To Slim or Not to Slim' from The Word Party by Richard Edwards (Lutterworth Press 1986) copyright © 1986 Richard Edwards. Used by permission of the author; Dick King-Smith: 'Should You Meet a Herd of Zebras' from Jungle Jingles (Doubleday 1990) included by A.P.Watt Ltd on behalf of Fox Busters Ltd.; Aislinn and Larry O'Loughlin: 'Wally the Wascally Weptile' from Worms Can't Fly by Aislinn and Larry O'Loughlin (Wolfhound Press 2000) copyright © 2000 Aislinn and Larry O'Loughlin. Used by permission of Wolfhound Press Ltd.; Michael Rosen: 'Charlie Chaplin Chewed a Cake' from Michael Rosen's ABC (Macdonald Young Books 1995) copyright © Michael Rosen 1995. Reprinted by permission of PFD on behalf of Michael Rosen; Coral Rumble: 'Why Barnacles Cling to Boats' copyright © Coral Rumble 1999, first published in Creatures, Teachers and Family Features (Macdonald Young Books), included by permission of the author; Nick Toczek: 'Talkative Cows' copyright © Nick Toczek 2000, first published in Never Stare at a Grizzly Bear (Macmillan Children's Books), included by permission of the author; Colin West: 'If a Ghoul is Fond of Ghoulash', 'A Proper Copper Kettle', 'Mr Lott's Allotment' and 'Ethel Read a Book' all copyright © Colin West, included by permission of the author.